For Ally, with big, big love

First published in hardback in the United Kingdom by HarperCollins *Children's Books* in 2023
HarperCollins *Children's Books* is a division of HarperCollins*Publishers* Ltd, 1 London Bridge Street, London SE1 9GF

www.harpercollins.co.uk

HarperCollins*Publishers*, Macken House, 39/40 Mayor Street Upper, Dublin 1, D01 C9W8, Ireland
ISBN: 978–0–00–841343–9

Text and illustrations copyright © Rob Biddulph 2023

1 3 5 7 9 10 8 6 4 2

Printed in Dubai

Five things to find in this book

A pearl in an oyster shell ☐
A tiny alien piloting a submarine ☐
A pirate fish ☐
A message in a bottle ☐
A diamond ring ☐

NTIC

Written and illustrated by

RobBiddulph

HarperCollins *Children's Books*

A mulberry sky
full of flashes
and rumbles.

An ocean alive

as it rises and tumbles.

And there, 'neath the waves of a stormy Atlantic,
There lives a blue whale, and his name is...

Gigantic.

This guy is unusual. He's different. He's odd.
The smallest blue whale in the whole of the pod.

His parents they love him, but hope all the same
That one day their son will grow into his name.

"Hey, titchy," taunts Titan. "If I were that small,
I'm not sure I'd feel like a whale at all!"

"In fact, little brother, I think you'd be wise
To make friends with Myrtle. She's much more your size."

He swims to the turtle
and smiles a shy smile.

"Hello there," she says.
"Let's hang out for a while."

So...

they leap...

and they dive...

and they dance...

and they play.

Big fun for small friends in the mouth of the bay.

Meanwhile,
plumes of seaweed
concealing their bulk,

It's Titan with buddies
Colossus and Hulk.

"Just look at
those pipsqueaks,"
he says with a frown.

"Let's get a bit closer,
see what's going down."

"Oh, wow," says Colossus, a smile on her chops,
"Gigantic's so good at those flippety flops!"

"Your brother," says Hulk, "is a talent, for sure!
I've not seen a whale do a tailspin before!"

"Nonsense!" says Titan.
"There can't be much to it!

"How hard can it be
if Gigantic can do it?

"I'll show those two shrimps
how a *real* whale can swim.

"And I'll do it BIGGER
and BETTER than him!"

"Wait," says Colossus. "Stay right where you are.
The sea in the bay is too shallow, by far."

Ignoring his friends, the determined young whale
Sets off through the blue with a swish of his tail.

Gigantic looks up as a shadow is cast.
"Be careful..." he warns, as his brother glides past.

"Watch this!" Titan says with a whopping wide grin.
He rotates his tail...

BUT IS GROUNDED, MID-SPIN!

So now we arrive at the turn of the tide.
Poor Titan is beached, lying stuck on his side.

"Quickly!" shouts Myrtle,
"This looks like bad news!
SMALL SEA LIFE, ASSEMBLE!
There's no time to lose!"

They come from the coral, the rocks and the caves,
The teenies and tinies that live 'neath the waves.
They dig and they scrape and they scoop and they suck,
All working as one to get Titan unstuck.

"Pull!" bellows Myrtle. "We haven't got long!"

"I'll help!" says Gigantic. "I'm small but I'm strong!"

He turns towards Titan, whose eyes swim with fear.
"Don't worry, big brother. I won't leave you here."

They heave and they drag and they haul and they strain,
Each one a small link in a much bigger chain.

The little blue whale pulls with all of his might...

And look! Titan's free!
What a wonderful sight!

Relieved, the huge whale
takes his leave of the bay.

Young Titan has learned
a hard lesson today.

And here comes Gigantic,
a smile on his face...

"Now show us that tailspin,
I bet that it's ace!"

"Gigantic," says Titan,
"I've been such a fool.
Enormously dim,
tiny-minded and cruel.

"I was blind to your talents,
but now I can see,
How hugely important
the small things can be.

"From now on I promise
to stop being mean.
I'll be the best brother
the world's ever seen."

Forget-me-not sky
    and a sun, warm and shiny.

An ocean alive,
filled with friends
large AND tiny.

Remember, your height doesn't set you apart.
What matters the most...

...is the size of your heart.

Draw a whale
with Rob

Scan this QR code and
learn how to draw
Gigantic and Myrtle
with Rob right now.